AGENTAmelia Hypno Hounds!

AGENT Amelia

Hypno Hounds!

MICHAEL BROAD

SCHOLASTIC INC.

First published in 2008 by Andersen Press Limited, 20 Vauxhall Bridge Road,
London SW1V 2SA

ISBN 978-0-545-51250-3

12 11 10 9 8 7 6   15 16 17/0

Printed in the U.S.A.   40

First Scholastic printing, October 2012

For Lisa

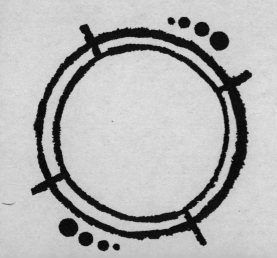

I'M AMELIA KIDD and I'm a secret agent.

Well, I'm not actually a secret agent. I don't work for the government or anything. But I've saved the world loads of times from evil geniuses and criminal masterminds. There are loads of them around if you know what to look for.

I'm really good at disguises. I make my own gadgets (which sometimes work), and I'm used to improvising in sticky situations—which you have to do all the time when you're a secret agent.

These are my Secret Agent Case Files.

The Case of the Hypno Hounds

During the summer, Mom rented a
cottage in the country for a whole
week. I was really looking forward to
the calm and quiet. I saw it as a
secret-agent vacation. A break from
saving the world.

Well, that was the plan. . . .

As Mom drove along the
winding country roads, I noticed that
we hadn't seen another person for

miles. As we passed through the village, it seemed deserted. I frowned over my sunglasses. The countryside was a bit *too* calm and quiet.

In the front yard of Bevil Cottage, I put down my suitcase and looked up at the sign.

"Why is it called *Bevil* Cottage?" I wondered aloud.

"Probably the name of the original owner or something," Mom suggested and continued up the path.

"Hmmm," I said. "Bevil" didn't sound like a real name to me. You have to be suspicious when you're a secret agent—even when you're on vacation.

I whipped out my magnifying glass and held it up to the sign and found the *B* in *Bevil* was newly painted. I could still see the old paint beneath. The *B* had been a *D*. The *real* name of the place we were staying was *Devil* Cottage!

When I caught Mom, she was at the cottage door speaking to a woman who seemed surprised to see us. She was wearing an apron, which made me think this was probably the housekeeper.

". . . and you didn't get my letter?" she said. "The one telling you not to come?"

Mom shook her head, and I
narrowed my eyes over my sunglasses.

"Then I think you'd better
come in," sighed the woman.

The housekeeper, Ms. Bloom,
explained that people were fleeing the
village out of sheer terror. She'd sent a
letter last week urging us not to come
for our own safety.

"Why?" Mom and I
said together.

"Because the DEVIL DOGS have returned!" she gasped dramatically.

"What's a devil dog?" I asked. Mom's teacup rattled nervously in her saucer.

"Legend tells of giant beasts who once roamed this area," whispered Ms. Bloom. "They stood as tall as a man, with massive teeth and big yellow eyes the size of dinner plates!"

Mom's eyes were pretty wide too as she lapped up the story. I wasn't convinced.

"Have you actually *seen* one of these devil dogs?" I asked casually.

"Well, not exactly," said Ms. Bloom. "But I've heard them howling in the night and found their paw prints in the morning. They were HUGE!"

"Then why do you stay here?" Mom asked. She seemed quite concerned.

"Because I have nowhere else to go," sighed the woman.

"We'll stay with you," I said quickly, before Mom had a chance to rush us back into the car.

Ms. Bloom seemed nice, and I wanted to get to the bottom of the devil dogs. "For the week anyway, eh, Mom?"

"Um, yes, of course!" Mom smiled nervously, reluctant to abandon the poor woman. Ms. Bloom was obviously relieved. She reassured us that it was perfectly safe during the day. She said that the devil dogs only come out at midnight but that the locks on the doors were very strong.

That night I checked the locks myself. Then I set up a surveillance station at my bedroom window.

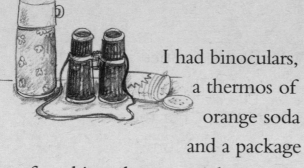 I had binoculars,
a thermos of
orange soda
and a package
of cookies—because nighttime
surveillance can be hungry work.

As the clock struck midnight, I
scanned the surrounding area with my
binoculars. The full moon was bright
and low and offered some light, but I
cursed myself for not pleading harder
for night-vision goggles last Christmas.

Then I heard a noise.

HOOOOOWL!

The howl seemed quite far off
and was answered by many more.

HOOOOOWL! HOOOOOWL!
HOOOOOWL!

As each howl grew nearer, I
suddenly saw a pack of dark shapes
charging across the neighboring field.
With the moon behind them, it was
impossible to see the creatures, but
the shadows they cast were long and
looked enormous!

When the shadows reached the
bushes on the near side of the field,
there was a frenzied rustling mixed
with ferocious growls and snarling.
Then the moon disappeared behind the
clouds. Everything went black.

Uh Oh!

I couldn't see anything through
my *non* night-vision binoculars. I
was pretty scared when I heard the
creatures prowling in the yard below.

But a secret agent can't let fear get the better of her, so I guarded the cottage until the beasts had gone.

In the morning, I got up early, crept downstairs, and searched the garden for clues. I found lots of trampled flowers and the same huge paw prints the housekeeper had mentioned. But there were no actual leads to go on.

Back indoors, Ms. Bloom was making breakfast. Mom was still in bed, so I saw this as a chance for a bit of informal interrogation.

"Why is this place called Devil Cottage?" I asked casually.

"How did you know that?" gasped the housekeeper.

"Oh, I just notice stuff," I replied.

"Devil Cottage was the *old* name," said Ms. Bloom. "From the days of the legend. But it scared people off, so I changed it to Bevil. Although now that the beasts have returned, I should probably change it back. . . ." She chuckled nervously and then burst into tears.

At this point, I was certain that Ms. Bloom had nothing to do with the devil dogs. You get a nose for these things when you're a secret agent.

And the distressed housekeeper made me even more determined to solve the midnight mystery.

"Morning!" chirped Mom. She skipped cheerily into the kitchen. She'd obviously slept through the howling hounds last night. "Now, what would you like to do today?"

"I'm afraid most of the local attractions have closed down," said

Ms. Bloom. "But there is a beautiful nature trail nearby. Just cut through the field, turn left at the animal shelter, and then—"

"Animal shelter!" I gasped. This was the lead I was looking for.

"Yes, Polly's Pooches!" said Ms. Bloom. "Do you like doggies?"

"Um, yeah!" I said. I turned to Mom. "Can we go and see the dogs?"

"Only if you promise not to beg for one like last time," Mom said firmly.

We'd visited an animal shelter last year, and I'd pestered Mom to adopt a retired police dog. I thought he'd come in handy as a tracker and sniffer on secret-agent missions. Mom said no.

As we walked across the field, I couldn't help wondering why no one else had made the connection between the devil dogs and the animal shelter.

It seemed pretty obvious to me. But this particular mystery was solved the moment we arrived.

Polly's Pooches were all teeny, tiny handbag dogs with ribbons in their hair!

Mom didn't have to worry about me begging for a handbag dog. They were all really adorable, but I couldn't keep one in my backpack. It might chew my gadgets and ruin my disguises.

The dinky dogs were definitely not devilish, but there could still be bigger dogs tucked somewhere out of sight. So I gave Mom the slip. While she was looking at a rosebush, I began snooping around. Eventually, I found a large barn that looked like the perfect place to hide a pack of huge hounds!

As I approached, the barn door creaked open. A woman stepped out. This was obviously Polly of Polly's Pooches. She had the exact same hairdo as her dogs. I quickly ducked behind the nearest kennel and watched as she locked the door with a padlock. Polly was looking around the whole time to make sure no one was watching. This made her my number one suspect.

When the woman walked away,
I slipped from my hiding place. I
approached the barn door. There was
no way I could get inside with the big
padlock in place, but
along the path leading
to the barn, I found
loads of paw prints
dried in the mud!

They were the
same huge prints I'd
seen in the cottage
yard!

I followed the tracks with my
magnifying glass. I noticed one of the
animals had veered off toward a
nearby bush, probably to relieve itself.
But when its tracks rejoined the pack
there was a paw print missing, as
though the creature had suddenly lost
a leg!

Animals don't just lose legs willy-nilly. I pulled out my extendable grabber-hand gadget and began rummaging around in the bush. Then I caught a glimpse of something red and shiny. I tugged it from the branches.

It was a rubber boot!

Hmmm? I thought. Then I turned the boot over to find a large paw-shaped mold stuck to the bottom. I pressed the boot into a dried muddy paw print. It was an exact fit.

"YOU THERE!" shrieked a high-pitched voice. "WHAT ARE YOU DOING?"

I turned to find Polly stomping toward me with a very angry look on her face.

"Hello!" I said cheerily. I quickly booted the boot back into the bush.

"Why are you snooping around here?" Polly demanded. "This is private property!"

"Er, I got lost," I sighed. I tried to look like a little girl lost—which is not easy to do in combat pants. I don't think Polly was convinced. Luckily Mom appeared, providing a handy escape route.

"I've been looking for you everywhere!" she sighed. "Are you ready to leave?"

"Yes, Mom," I smiled. I skipped past a furious Polly. "But I'll be back!" I mumbled under my breath.

I didn't pack many disguises for the vacation, so that night I had to borrow Ms. Bloom's cape and hat. Luckily they were both dark blue and cloaked my almost-midnight dash across the field.

When I reached Polly's barn, the
door was unlocked. I poked my head
inside and was relieved not to have it
bitten off by a pack of massive dogs.
The barn was completely empty
except for a strange structure at one
end. I slipped inside to take a closer
look.

It was a huge cardboard wheel
with a whirly pattern painted on the
front like a giant lollipop! I stepped
up to the structure, turned the wheel
a little, and then peered around the
back.

Behind the wheel, there was a
table with a map of the whole village
with areas colored in where people
had moved out. Most of the map was
colored. In fact, Devil Cottage seemed
to be the only place left.

Under the map was a blueprint for a giant animal shelter the exact size of the village and a diagram for a giant whirly wheel the size of a football field! None of this made much sense. Then I lifted the blueprint to find a picture of the world cut from an atlas.

It had the words "I want to take this over!" scribbled above it.

"Typical!" I thought.

Suddenly I heard someone approaching the barn. I quickly crept into the hayloft and hid behind a bale of straw. Moments later, Polly barged through the door pushing a wheelbarrow full of rubber boots. Dozens of dinky dogs followed her.

Polly whistled, and the animals lined up and waited patiently. Polly fixed the tall boots on their dinky legs. Then she stepped away and spun the giant whirly wheel.

I watched from above as the cute fluffy pooches stared at the spinning pattern. They all tilted their heads as the wheel whizzed around.

Then each dog twitched and began snarling, growling, and

HOOOOOWLING!

Polly smiled a wicked smile. She whistled through her fingers and then flung her arms in the air dramatically.

"Run, my pretties! RUN!" she shrieked. The mini devil dogs hobbled around and bounded from the barn in their strange red boots.

They looked scary *and* silly all at the same time.

Evil geniuses and criminal masterminds often like to rant about their plans for world domination. I've heard *loads* of them. And they don't always need an audience. Some are quite happy to rant to themselves!

"When my hounds have cleared the village, I'll take over the WHOLE WORLD with MILLIONS of devil dogs and a GIANT hypno wheel," Polly hissed, pacing up and down like a lunatic.

That explained the plans for a huge animal shelter. Then I remembered that Devil Cottage was the only place left on the map. I guessed the madwoman had probably sent the hounds there. Luckily Polly was too busy ranting to see me climb down from the hayloft and creep away.

The dogs moved surprisingly fast across the field in their funky footwear. I managed to catch up with them as they neared the bushes near Devil Cottage. The only thing I could think to do was whistle through my fingers like Polly had done. Suddenly, the snarling pooches stopped and hobbled around.

HOOOOOWL! HOOOOOWL!

HOOOOOWL!

Uh Oh!

The hypno hounds suddenly bounded after me. I took off across the field.

When I reached the barn, the dogs were snapping at my heels. I barged past Polly, who was still ranting and pacing. I spun the hypno wheel in the opposite direction.

The dogs screeched to a halt and tilted their heads. Suddenly, they turned all cute again.

"MY DEVIL DOGS!" yelled
Polly, striding toward me.

"They're not DEVIL DOGS!" I
yelled back. "They're HANDBAG
HOUNDS!"

"We'll see about that!" she growled, grabbing the other side of the wheel.

Polly tugged the wheel one way. I tugged it back. This tug-of-wheel went on for a quite a long time. As the wheel spun back and forth, the poor dogs sat in the middle of the barn twitching from cute to crazed and crazed to cute.

My arms were getting tired from all the tugging when Polly suddenly let go. She leaped around the wheel to grab me, but as she lunged, she happened to glance sideways. She froze like a statuc. Polly gazed at the hypno wheel, tilted her head, and twitched. Then she began snarling, growling, and

HOOOOOWLING!

I wasn't sure what to do, so I whistled through my fingers again.

Polly immediately pulled on a pair of boots, fled the barn, and took off across the field like a *human* devil dog. I was about to race after her when I saw the poor pooches peering up at me. I decided to take care of them first.

Luckily the dogs were in cute mode. To make sure they stayed that way, I pulled down the hypno wheel and broke it in half with a well-aimed karate kick.

Then I released each of the bewildered beasts from their red rubber boots.

By the time I reached the cottage, I found Ms. Bloom in the garden shooing Polly out of her flower beds with a broom. The housekeeper obviously had things under control. I hid behind the hedge until the police arrived to take Polly away.

She was yelling, "I'm a DEVIL DOG!" and howling at the top of her lungs.

You can't take credit for saving the world when you're a secret agent. When Ms. Bloom went back inside and turned out the lights, I crept through the garden and snuck back into my room.

I tried to look surprised when the housekeeper told us the story the next morning.

". . . and Polly was sniffing around my rosebushes!" gasped Ms. Bloom. "So I gave her a good WALLOP with my broom and called the police. And it turned out that *she* was behind the devil dogs! Something to do with rubber boot paw prints or something?"

"What a relief!" said Mom.

I smiled behind my sunglasses.

"Anyway, I've been on the phone all morning. People are already moving back to the village," added Ms. Bloom, excitedly. "Oh, and they've asked me to look after the dogs until homes can be found. . . ."

"Can I help?" I asked, sitting up eagerly. A calm and quiet vacation isn't really for me. I'd rather keep busy. And I'd grown quite fond of those cute little devil dogs. I just had to make sure they stayed away from my backpack!

The Case of the Sneaky Scientist

I was really looking forward to our first science lab at school. I figured I'd learn something that could help my secret-agent activities. But the new teacher, Mr. Gumble, had other ideas.

"Perfume and stink bombs!" he declared, handing out worksheets to the class.

The girls were given a pink worksheet called *How To Make Perfume*. The boys were given a blue worksheet called *How to Make a Stink Bomb*. I didn't want to make perfume *or* a stink bomb, so I put my hand up.

"Amelia Kidd?" said Mr. Gumble, looking down at the attendance book.

"Um, is there a worksheet called *How to Make a Smoke Bomb*?" I asked. A smoke bomb might come in handy on secret-agent missions, to create a diversion or conceal a quick getaway.

The teacher obviously thought I was joking. He rolled his eyes disapprovingly.

"A *smoke* bomb!" scoffed Trudy Hart. "What a typically stupid idea!"

"Oh, mind your own business," I said.

Trudy is my arch nemesis at school. She's not an evil genius or a criminal mastermind. But she *is* really annoying. Trudy's also very popular and sees herself as a bit of a school celebrity.

"I'm going to create my own perfume called *Love Hart*," Trudy bragged to her two sidekicks. "A brand-new scent that will smell almost as pretty as me!"

"Then you might want the stink bomb worksheet," I chuckled.

"Just for that, I'm going to *ban* you from buying it!" snapped Trudy.

"Good!" I said. "I wouldn't want to smell like *you* anyway—"

"Everyone needs to get into pairs for this project," interrupted Mr. Gumble. He was glaring at Trudy and me. "And as you two already have such good *chemistry*, I think you should make very interesting lab partners."

"Huh?" I said, as Trudy's jaw dropped.

After the class had shuffled around in a chorus of chair shrieks, each pair got a measuring beaker and a rack filled with test tubes.

The girls' racks were filled with
scented oils, and the boys' racks were
filled with something murky and
unpleasant looking.

Mr. Gumble wrote a bunch of
instructions and diagrams on the
whiteboard. Then he explained that
one student would do the lab
experiment while the other took
notes.

"I don't want your fingers contaminating the creation of *Love Hart*. It might end up smelling like unpopularity," sniffed Trudy. She gathered the apparatus to her side of the desk. "But I will allow you to make notes while I select the formula."

"Whatever," I sighed. Science lab had turned out to be the worst class ever.

"I shall begin with a hint of rose," said Trudy, lifting a test tube from the rack and waving it under her nose. Then she tipped half of the oil into the beaker and gazed at it forlornly. "I think roses will remind everyone of my beautiful rosy cheeks."

I was about to say something about Trudy's thorny personality, when I noticed Mr. Gumble acting very suspiciously at his desk.

He was fiddling inside his very large briefcase and peering over the top to make sure no one was watching.

Uh Oh!

Last week I'd run a background check on Mr. Gumble. I'd also carried out basic surveillance on him, as I do with all new teachers. And I'd been particularly vigilant because scientists are really clever and often have thoughts of taking over the world.

At the time, I was convinced the new science teacher was fine and not an evil genius or a criminal mastermind. But judging by his shifty behavior and the oversized briefcase, I suspected Mr. Gumble had slipped under my radar.

You can't trust scientists!

I was wearing sunglasses under my safety goggles, so Mr. Gumble couldn't see me watching as he carefully closed the case and glanced around the room. He also didn't notice my eyes narrow when he tiptoed through the door clutching his briefcase!

Teachers aren't supposed to leave classrooms unattended unless it's an emergency. Even then, they usually say where they're going and warn the class that the teacher in the next room will be looking in. Mr. Gumble just slid away without a word. He was *definitely* up to something.

"Um, I just need to ask the teacher a question," I said. I slipped out of my seat and rummaged inside my backpack under the desk. I pulled out the first wig I laid my hands on and tucked it in the pocket of my combat pants.

"But who
will record my
glorious creation?"
Trudy demanded.

"Do it yourself, rosy cheeks!" I
said. Then I chased after the suspect
scientist.

I stepped into the hall just as
Mr. Gumble turned the corner. I
sprinted after him and skidded to a
halt before the turn. When I peeped
around the corner, the teacher was
hanging up his lab coat and ducking
out through the main doors.

Mr. Gumble
was leaving the
school grounds!

I knew I wouldn't
get far sneaking out of
school looking like a kid,
so I grabbed the lab coat
and pulled it on. The
wig I'd chosen turned
out to be frizzy disco hair. Lots of
mad scientists have crazy hairdos, so I
pulled that on too.

Stepping off school property, I did get a few odd looks from people, but I ignored them and followed Mr. Gumble. He was walking very fast, but I'm used to tracking suspects. I managed to keep up without being spotted.

The sneaky scientist shot into the local supermarket, so I slipped in after him. We both took carts. I made sure to stay low and keep my distance as I followed him through the aisles.

I didn't believe for one minute that the teacher had skipped out of class to do grocery shopping. He wouldn't need a huge briefcase for that. This made me think that whatever he was up to was probably inside the case!

Mr. Gumble stopped in the breakfast cereal aisle. He looked around suspiciously and then began loading his cart with box after box of SugarPop Hoops. He was drawing lots of attention from the other shoppers.

I've been on patrol in a supermarket before. I know you have to shop and put different stuff in your cart to pass for a regular shopper.

Watching from behind a box of Oaty Lumps, I realized Mr. Gumble was terrible at deception. I decided I could use this to my advantage and nab the briefcase!

The teacher was becoming more and more flustered as the other shoppers gave him strange looks. I ran down the aisle with my cart. I positioned myself on the side for a high-speed grab.

Ducking down,
I grabbed for the
briefcase as the cart
zoomed past. In the same
moment, Mr. Gumble whipped *his*
cart around, causing me to swerve and
crash into the nearest display.

CRASH!

BOING!

BOING!

BOING!

Luckily it was a display of toilet paper rolls that provided a soft, bouncy landing.

Standing up and adjusting my wig, I couldn't see Mr. Gumble because a crowd had gathered around me making a fuss. I didn't have time for lengthy explanations, so I made use of my disguise.

"Everybody out of the way, I'm
a doctor!" I yelled. I barged through
the crowd.

Running down the aisle, I saw Mr. Gumble leaving the checkout lane with four bags of groceries. When I say groceries, I mean a dozen boxes of SugarPop Hoops! I slipped past the cashier and followed the teacher back to the street.

This was turning into a very complicated mission, but I tried to stay focused.

If Mr. Gumble wasn't planning anything tricky *in* the supermarket, then he was planning something tricky with what he'd *bought* from the supermarket *and* the contents of his suspiciously large briefcase . . . probably.

My suspect was heading back into school, so I stayed by the gates and

spied through the bars as he hurried up
the sidewalk. But instead of entering
the building, he ducked around the side
to where the teachers park their cars.

I followed, using the bushes for
cover. I watched as Mr. Gumble
opened the trunk of his car. He began
filling it with SugarPop Hoops.

I don't mean he loaded the bags of groceries into the trunk. He was actually opening the boxes and *pouring* the cereal. He acted like the car was a giant breakfast bowl!

CHOMP!

CHOMP!

CHOMP!

From the bushes, I could hear chomping sounds coming from the trunk, which was bouncing up and down as some mysterious creature ate the cereal! I couldn't see what it was, but I immediately suspected a diabolical experiment.

Evil scientists can't resist a diabolical experiment.

I had to confront the strange Dr. Frankenstein and find out what kind of monster was lurking in his car.

But without my trusty backpack, I had
no gadgets to defend myself.

When you're a secret agent, you
have to improvise in sticky situations.
I grabbed the nearest thing that could
deliver a good wallop. Unfortunately
the nearest thing was a sunflower. But
the stem was stiff and the head was
heavy and I didn't really have a
choice.

I crept along the row of parked vehicles with the sunflower. I tiptoed along the side of Mr. Gumble's car. With the trunk lid up, the teacher couldn't see me. This was handy, because a girl with a giant flower needs all the cover she can get.

"AHA!" I yelled, leaping into the open and wielding my floral weapon.

"ARGH!" yelled Mr. Gumble, hiding behind the SugarPop Hoop box.

This wasn't the reaction I was
expecting, but I stood my ground.

"I'm not sure *exactly* what you're
up to, Gumble," I said. I waved the
flower at him. "But you're not going
to get away with it!"

"Amelia Kidd?" frowned the teacher. He lowered the cereal box. "Is that you?"

"Well . . . yes, actually!" I said. My cover was blown, so I pulled the wig off and shoved it in my pocket.

But I wasn't going to let him change the subject that easily. "As I was saying, I'm here to stop you—"

"And is that my lab coat?" Mr. Gumble asked uncertainly.

"Er, yes," I said. I pulled off the lab coat and dumped it on the floor.

I couldn't figure out what was going on. Evil geniuses and criminal masterminds usually turn pretty nasty when confronted. Or they try to make a quick getaway. Or they start ranting about their fiendish plans.

Mr. Gumble just seemed startled and a bit confused.

"Pay attention!" I yelled, before he could interrupt again. "I'm here to stop you from taking over the world!"

"Taking over the world?" he gasped.

"Yes," I said. I jabbed the sunflower in the direction of the trunk. "You're planning to take over the world using this diabolical monstrosity. . . ." I glanced into the trunk for the first time. I saw a dozen balls of pink fluff peering back at me.

"They're not monsters," said Mr. Gumble. He seemed a bit offended.

"What are they then?" I frowned. "Man-eating pom-poms?"

"I don't know what they are," Mr. Gumble confessed. "They grew by accident in my lab. But they don't eat people," he added quickly, waving the cereal box. "They eat SugarPop Hoops."

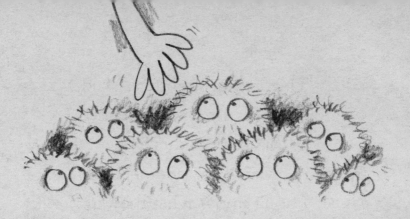

I propped my sunflower against
the car, reached cautiously into the
trunk, and picked up one of the small
fluffy creatures. It was warm in my
hand and giggled when I tickled
its fur.

"My wife usually looks after them, but she's visiting her mother," explained Mr. Gumble. "So I had to bring them to school for their morning feeding. You see, we have no children of our own and have grown awfully fond of them. . . ."

"Can I feed them?" I asked. Mr. Gumble shrugged and handed me the last box of SugarPop Hoops. "When the scientific world discovers that I've accidentally created a new species, they'll want to take them away," he said sadly. "They'll put them in a cage and poke and prod them. . . ."

"You can't trust scientists," I said, shaking the cereal into the trunk. The pink, fluffy creatures jumped up and down excitedly as they chomped on their food. "But how will they find out you have them?"

"When you tell people, of course," said Mr. Gumble. "Word will spread very quickly."

"Oh, I won't tell anyone," I said casually.

"You won't?" gasped the teacher.

"No," I said. I knew that my first impression of Mr. Gumble had been correct. He wasn't an evil genius or a criminal mastermind. "As long as you promise not to take over the world with them."

"Why would I want to take over the world?" he frowned.

"I don't know," I said. "But I've met a *lot* of people who do. . . ."

I suddenly realized I'd said too much. For a moment it looked as though Mr. Gumble was about to quiz me about *my* part in all this. But then he nodded and smiled kindly.

"I promise not to take over the world," he said, holding out his hand.

As we shook hands to seal the deal, I could tell the teacher and I had an understanding.

I wouldn't mention his adopted pom-poms, and he wouldn't mention my secret-agent activities.

With the fluffy creatures fed, Mr. Gumble opened his large briefcase. They jumped in one by one. I gathered the empty cereal boxes and stuffed them in the shopping bags for recycling.

Then the teacher pulled on his lab coat and led me back to class.

The science room was very different from the one we'd left behind!

Standing in the doorway, I
noticed that the first difference was the
noise. All of my classmates were yelling
and screaming. The second difference
was the smell, which was REALLY
bad. It reminded me of rotten eggs and
moldy cabbage mixed with perfume.

"SILENCE!" roared an angry voice behind us.

Mr. Gumble and I jumped. The principal, Mrs. Marshall, stormed into the classroom. Then everything immediately went quiet. But the lab still smelled like a landfill.

"What on earth is going on in here?" Mrs. Marshall demanded.

She scanned the room and then
turned to Mr. Gumble for the answer.
"I saw you strolling down the
corridor. I can only assume you have
an excellent excuse for leaving the
classroom unattended?"

I looked up at Mr. Gumble. He had a familiar startled expression on his face. It was the same expression he wore when I confronted him with the sunflower. I could tell he was about to confess again!

I didn't want the pom-poms to get poked and prodded, so I quickly spoke up.

"It was an *emergency*, Mrs. Marshall!" I gasped. I remembered the rule about unattended classrooms.

Then I remembered I was still holding the grocery bags filled with empty cereal boxes. "I ate too many SugarPop Hoops and was sick!"

"Oh," said the principal. She took a bag and peered inside.

"Oh, dear!"

Mrs. Marshall bought the story. She left Mr. Gumble in charge. The teacher gave me a grateful nod as he placed the briefcase carefully on his desk. Then he took control of the classroom.

I went back to my seat next to
Trudy and lifted the beaker of *Love
Hart* to my nose.

"URGH!" I shuddered. "Is *this*
what you smell like?"

"Of course not, you unpopular
fool!" growled Trudy. She glared at me
as though everything was my fault.
"The boys poured something *else* into
the beaker, something that smelled
like manure!"

"Well, manure *is* very good for roses," I smiled. I looked at Trudy's furious face, which was now scarlet with rage. "Perhaps that explains why your rosy cheeks are positively blooming!"

The Case of the Terrible Teddies

"I just can't understand why you're
still sulking about it!" said Mom, as we
entered the local department store.
"We're here now, and
it's not as though
you're likely to
need anything."
        "Hmph!"
I said,
folding my
arms defiantly.

We'd spent the whole car ride arguing about my backpack. Mom insisted that it was too big and heavy for a shopping trip. I'd failed to offer a good enough reason why I needed it.

I couldn't tell Mom that the bag was full of secret-agent stuff or that you never know when an evil genius or criminal mastermind might try to take over the world. So my faithful backpack got left behind.

"Now, what is it we're looking for again?" Mom asked cheerily. She wanted to change the subject. "A teddy bear and a pair of roller skates?"

"Turbo Ted," I sighed. "A remote-control teddy bear *on* roller skates."

"Oh, yes," Mom smirked, "I remember now. . . ." Mom hadn't *really* forgotten. She was just trying to get me talking.

My cousin had been going on and on all week about getting Turbo Ted for his birthday. It was the latest toy craze for younger kids.

Unfortunately, when we found the Turbo Ted display, it was empty. There was not a single bear for sale. Dozens of disappointed kids gathered around. One of the disappointed kids was much bigger than the rest, and she was making a much bigger fuss!

"THIS IS UNACCEPTABLE!"
she squealed.

Trudy Hart was standing next to the display with her tired-looking dad. She was causing a bit of a scene. The store manager was trying to calm her down. He wasn't having much success.

"I'm terribly sorry, miss," he said. "But we do have many other nice things for a sophisticated young lady. I'm sure you're too grown up to play with teddy bears anyway. . . ."

Trudy's dad gasped and took a step back.

"I don't *play* with them, you silly little man," growled Trudy. "I *collect* them!"

"Oh," gulped the manager. "I'm sure I didn't mean . . ."

"It's a very *grown-up* and intellectual hobby," interrupted Trudy. "My teddy bear collection is one of the finest in the world. You've just ruined my reputation with your incompetence!"

With this Trudy stormed away, leaving the manager with his mouth hanging open.

"Those roller-skating teddies must be awfully popular to sell out so quickly," said Mom, stepping up to the manager. "Do you have any idea when they'll be back in stock?"

"That's the problem, madam," he said, scratching his head. "Fifty new Turbo Teds arrived this morning. We haven't sold a single one! The entire stock just vanished!"

I lowered my sunglasses when I heard the word *vanished*. In my experience, things never just vanish. There's always *someone* behind the vanishing.

"You mean
they were stolen?"
I asked casually.

"No," said the
manager. "The
head of security
has been
through all the security camera tapes.
He said the bears were there one
minute and gone the next. It's a
complete mystery!"

Very suspicious, I thought.

I was just wondering whether
the missing teddies warranted an
investigation when
I saw something
whiz by out
of the corner
of my eye.

I only caught a brief glimpse, but it looked suspiciously like a small bear on roller skates!

"I suppose we'll have to find something else for your cousin," Mom sighed. "I know he'll be very disappointed, but I'm sure if we put our heads together, we can think of something nice."

I frowned at the "we" part. I couldn't carry out an investigation with Mom tagging along. And I knew she'd find me if I gave her the slip. So I needed a really good excuse to go off on my own.

"Can I have a look in the Girly Girl clothing section?" I asked. Mom would definitely encourage my showing an interest in pretty dresses instead of the usual combat gear.

"Yes, of course!" Mom gasped. She flapped her hands eagerly. "Off you go, darling!"

I immediately took off down the aisle toward the girls' section. Without my backpack, I was planning to dress up in a pink frilly dress for my disguise. It would be uncomfortable, but Mom wouldn't recognize me. No one else would suspect a girly girl of being a secret agent.

Unfortunately, I had to abandon that plan the moment I arrived at Girly Girl.

"Well, I think they're all UGLY!" yelled a familiar voice from a sea of frills and bows. "I wouldn't be seen dead in any of them. Don't you know that the customer is *always* right?!?"

I'd managed to avoid Trudy Hart back at the bear display, and I definitely didn't have time for her now. So I ducked into the nearest aisle and found myself in the *men's* clothing section!

A secret agent can't afford to be choosy when she needs a quick disguise. I rummaged through the racks for something I could work with. Eventually I pulled on a brown overcoat. Then I popped a bowler hat on my head and grabbed an umbrella.

A quick glance in the mirror revealed a rather convincing businessman.

I was adjusting my bowler, which was a bit too big, when I heard a commotion at the checkout lane. The customers in line were searching their pockets and handbags while the store staff looked bewildered.

"My wallet!" said one man.

"My purse!" said a woman.

It looked as though most of the customers in the line had lost their money. This was a lot of picked pockets for one department store! There would have to be a whole gang of pickpockets working the place. This was a bit of an odd coincidence, considering the missing Turbo Teds.

Unless . . .

I scanned the store and saw a
small furry paw reach into a woman's
handbag and pull out her wallet!
Nearby another paw appeared from a
clothes rack and reached into a man's
coat. Everywhere I
looked, I saw little furry
arms in pockets and
handbags. Brown
blurs were
whizzing all
over the place.

The Turbo
Teds were robbing
the place!

One of the bears whizzed
past my legs with a pink purse in its
paws. I took off after it, chasing it

through the aisles as
its fuzzy, brown
legs skated like
mad. The toy

weaved in and out of
clothes racks. It was getting away, so I
leapt forward, swung my umbrella, and
hooked the cuddly
crook around
the waist.

"Gotcha!" I said. I immediately flicked the switch on its back to Off.

Then I plucked the purse from its paws and inspected the fuzzy bandit. I suspected someone had programmed the toys and sent them on a crime spree. But there were no marks or modifications. It looked like a regular Turbo Ted.

A regular *remote-control* Turbo Ted!

Someone was *controlling* the
burglar bears from a distance.

The department store was huge
and full of people moving around.
Trying to spot a suspicious character
among the masses was like finding a
needle in a haystack. Then I looked up
and saw a security camera buzzing
over my head.

"Aha!" I said. I shoved the bear headfirst into the clothes rack.

The manager said the security guard hadn't seen the bears disappear, but he wasn't a secret agent with an eye for evil geniuses and criminal masterminds. If I could just find a way to view those security tapes. . . .

"THIEF!" shrieked a familiar voice. "That short man has my pretty pink purse!"

Uh Oh!

I quickly whipped the umbrella handle under my nose to conceal my face from Trudy. Before I could escape, the store manager appeared from behind and grabbed my arm firmly.

"Gotcha!" he said, taking the purse and handing it to my fuming foe.

Trudy snatched the purse. She was about to tell the manager off again when I suddenly knew how I could get in to see the security tapes. I quickly fished around in my pocket and pulled out my library card.

"Excellent work!" I said, in my deepest, most official voice. "Very well done!"

"Excuse me?" said the manager.

"I'm the Regional, er, Security Supervisory, er, Manager!" I said waving my library card in his face. "I got a call from headquarters saying you have a security problem in your store?"

"Well, yes," frowned the manager. "But—"

"No time to explain," I said, pocketing the card and tugging my arm free. "You must take me to your head of security immediately!"

"But what about me?" Trudy demanded. "I'm a victim of crime!"

"Pardon me, miss," I said. "You dropped your purse over by the frilly underwear. I was simply attempting to return it. Perhaps you should spend more time guarding your things and less time yelling at people!"

The store manager stifled a smirk as he led me to the security guard's office. He introduced me as the Regional Security Supervisory Manager, which was handy because I'd forgotten the made-up title I'd told him.

"So you need to view the tapes?" said the security guard after the manager left.

"Yes," I said. "Please start with the Turbo Ted display from earlier today."

The man fiddled with a couple of buttons and then pointed to one of the monitors. But instead of the teddy display, the screen showed a close-up of the men's clothing section, with

me assembling my businessman disguise!

Uh Oh!

It was then that I took a closer look at the joysticks lined up along his desk. At first I'd assumed they were there to operate the security cameras. After a closer look, I realized they were not actually connected to cameras. They were *remote-control* joysticks!

"You're working the cuddly crooks!" I said. I was annoyed that I hadn't figured it out earlier. "And you're using the security cameras to direct them from a distance!"

"Yes," said the security guard, proudly. "And this is only the beginning!"

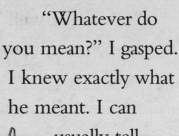

"Whatever do you mean?" I gasped. I knew exactly what he meant. I can usually tell when a taking-over-the-world rant is coming. I had to stall for time while I worked out a plan.

"Once my bears have stolen enough purses and wallets, I'll buy an army of Turbo Teds," he said, pointing to the pickpockets on the monitors. "And soon I'll have enough to rob the whole world!"

"You won't get away with it!" I said.

"Oh, yes, I will!" he laughed. Then he began tugging and jerking the joysticks.

At first I thought he was ignoring me and carrying on with the pickpocketing. Then I heard a strange noise thundering down the corridor. I realized he'd guided the teddy bears to the office!

The rumbling reached the room, and the door burst open. Then fifty fluffy bears zoomed inside with wallets and purses. They began circling my legs like I was standing in the center of a tiny roller rink.

ZOOM!

ZOOM!

ZOOM!

The security guard
snatched the loot from
each of the bears and
stuffed it in a
sack. Then he
threw the sack
over his shoulder,
laughed like a
maniac, and bolted
from the office.

The Turbo Teds had picked up
so much speed that I
couldn't step through them.
I pulled off my overcoat and
threw it over the toy
tornado. Most of the bears
became tangled in the coat. They
tumbled across the room and landed
in a heap against the wall.

The rest I slapped
away using my umbrella
like a hockey stick.

WHACK!

WHACK!

WHACK!

I ran to the camera controls and
saw the security guard walking very
quickly through the store. Then I
noticed there were still a few remote-
control bears in the store. I began
wiggling the joysticks to get them to
move.

Once I'd figured out the
joysticks, I sent the skaters after the
guard. I made them weave in and out
of his legs. The bears slowed him
down, but he was still getting away, so
I took off after him.

Back in the store, I realized I was no longer in disguise. The coat and the umbrella were in the office. All I had left was the bowler hat. It must have looked pretty odd on its own, so I slipped it off.

I ducked down as I ran through the aisles. I couldn't risk drawing attention to myself dressed as me. The guard was nearing the exit doors. If I didn't act fast, he would escape with the loot.

I couldn't shout out, because no one would suspect a security guard of picking pockets. I had no backpack, and that meant no gadgets to help me.

All I had was a silly bowler hat that wasn't even mine. . . .

Then I had an idea. I paused to turn the hat over in my hands.

As I suspected, there was an electronic security tag on the inside. No one could take the hat from the store because alarms would go off as it passed through the sensors!

With the guard approaching the exit doors, I knew I only had one shot. I made a few practice flicks with my wrist, and then I threw the hat like a Frisbee.

The bowler flew through the air like a black flying saucer. It soared over the heads of the shoppers and through the sensors as the guard approached. It was a better shot than I'd hoped. It clipped his head and knocked his cap over his eyes.

WA! WA! WA!

The store alarms screamed, and all the shoppers turned to see the guard bump blindly into the doors before staggering back into the store. Just then, a stray bear rolled under his legs. The crook tripped and landed on his bottom.

"My wallet!" yelled one man.

"My purse!" shrieked a woman.

The loot sack had fallen open, spilling its contents over the floor. A crowd of angry shoppers quickly gathered around the crook. Moments later, the store manager appeared and pulled the guard to his feet.

"Has anyone seen the Regional Security Supervisory Manager?" he asked. "He's a little man with an umbrella and a bowler?"

Needless to say, no one had seen him. The store manager called the police, and the dazed guard was taken away. He was mumbling about little girls and bears. He didn't make any sense to anyone.

As the crowd left with their purses and wallets, Trudy stormed toward the manager with her dad. She picked up the stray Turbo Ted that had tripped the crook. She waved it at the manager.

"So you had them in stock the whole time!" she growled.

"Er, I'm not sure where this one came from," said the manager. He frowned at the bear.

"But I'd be happy to let you have it, to apologize for any inconvenience. I'm sure we can find the joystick. . . . "

"Are you crazy?" Trudy squealed. "It's worth NOTHING if it's not still in the box!"

Trudy Hart stomped out of the department store. She left without ever knowing I was there, because this time I was hiding behind a rack of puffy pink dresses.

"There you are!" said Mom, stepping through the aisle. "Did you find anything you like?"

"No!" I gasped. I backed
away from the dresses
before she insisted on
buying one.

"Me neither," Mom sighed. "It's
such a shame about those roller-
skating bears. . . . "

"THE TURBO TEDS?" I yelled,
loud enough for the manager to hear.

"IF ONLY THEY HAD *ONE* IN STOCK! I'M SURE WE DON'T CARE IF IT'S IN A BOX OR NOT. . . ."

Mom had obviously missed all the drama and didn't understand why I was shouting. So I just raised an eyebrow and tried to look surprised when the manager walked over to us.

He was smiling and holding up my cousin's birthday present.